ACROSS THE BAY

To my mother, who did miracles to raise five kids on her own.
To Brenda, Carmencita, and a magical place I grew up
called Puerto Rico—CA

PENGUIN WORKSHOP
An Imprint of Penguin Random House LLC, New York

Penguin supports copyright. Copyright fuels creativity, encourages diverse voices, promotes free speech, and creates a vibrant culture. Thank you for buying an authorized edition of this book and for complying with copyright laws by not reproducing, scanning, or distributing any part of it in any form without permission. You are supporting writers and allowing Penguin to continue to publish books for every reader.

Copyright © 2019 by Carlos Aponte. All rights reserved. Published by Penguin Workshop, an imprint of Penguin Random House LLC, New York. PENGUIN and PENGUIN WORKSHOP are trademarks of Penguin Books Ltd, and the W colophon is a registered trademark of Penguin Random House LLC. Manufactured in China.

Visit us online at www.penguinrandomhouse.com.

Library of Congress Cataloging-in-Publication Data is available upon request.

ISBN 9781524786625   10 9 8 7 6 5 4 3 2 1

ACROSS THE BAY

WRITTEN AND ILLUSTRATED BY CARLOS APONTE

PENGUIN WORKSHOP

Carlitos lived in the town of Cataño, across the bay from the capital. Mango, avocado, and banana trees grew in every yard. These were the pride of the people.

Most of the families in Carlitos's town looked the same. His family didn't look like the others.

Carlitos lived in a colorful house with his mother Carmen, his abuela, and Coco the cat. Fresh azucenas filled every room. These were Abuela's favorite flowers.

Carlitos loved the town of Cataño. But he did not like the barbershop.

"Buenas días, Doña Carmen!" said Francisco the barber.

"Buenas días, Francisco," said Carlitos's mother. "Just a trim for my handsome little man."

Carlitos blushed.

"And if you finish first," said Carmen to her son, "I'll be across the street at the bcauty salon."

Carmen paid the barber, blew her son a kiss, and left the barbershop.

Carlitos took a seat and waited his turn, next to the fathers and sons.

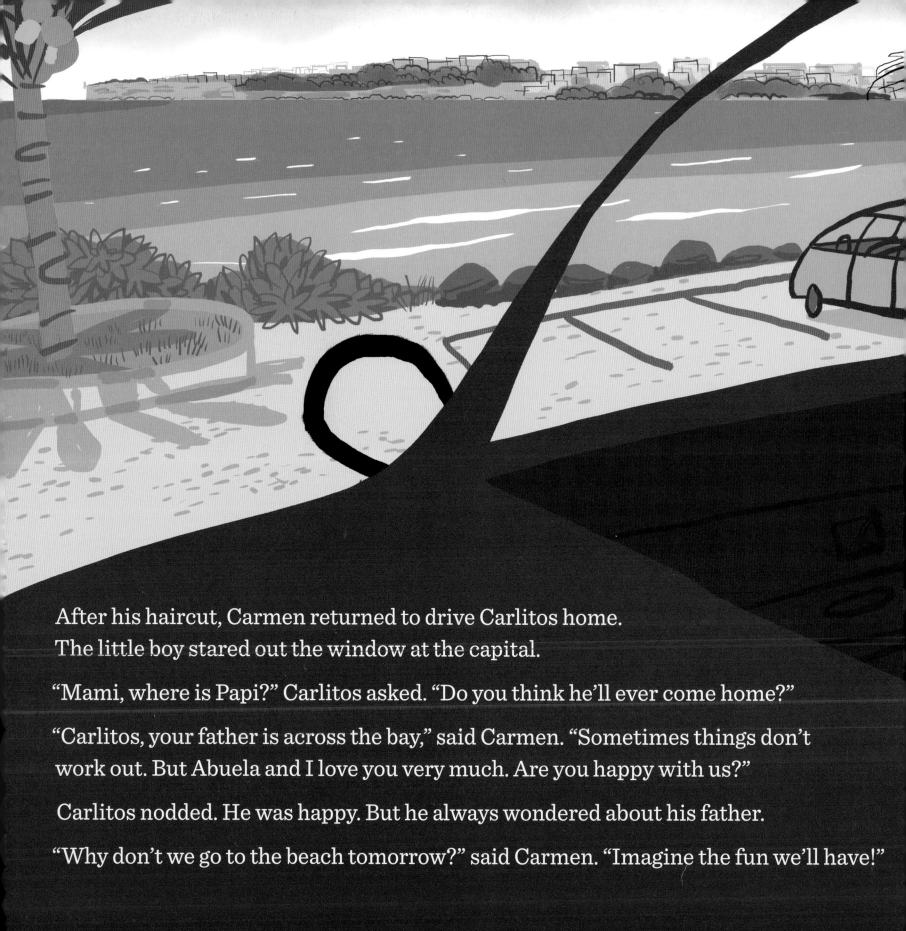

After his haircut, Carmen returned to drive Carlitos home.
The little boy stared out the window at the capital.

"Mami, where is Papi?" Carlitos asked. "Do you think he'll ever come home?"

"Carlitos, your father is across the bay," said Carmen. "Sometimes things don't work out. But Abuela and I love you very much. Are you happy with us?"

Carlitos nodded. He was happy. But he always wondered about his father.

"Why don't we go to the beach tomorrow?" said Carmen. "Imagine the fun we'll have!"

At home, Carlitos opened a small wooden box he kept in his dresser.
Under a pile of cards and comics, he found an old photo of his father.

"I'll find you, Papi," the little boy said, tucking the photo in his pocket.

Next, he grabbed some money Abuela had slipped under his pillow.
He tiptoed quietly out the front door . . . and straight to the ferry terminal.

Carlitos bought a ticket and sat by the window.

So far, so good, he thought.

On the boat ride, the boy heard *whoosh* and *splash* as the ferry cut through the waves. The ancient city of Old San Juan grew bigger and bigger.

The trip was short, but it felt like a long voyage. When he entered the city, it looked like a maze.

On a sunny corner, Carlitos approached a piragüera shaving iced treats.

"Excuse me," said the boy. "Do you know this man?" He showed the ice vendor the photo.

"No," said the vendor. "But there is a woman named Cassandra who feeds stray cats by the cathedral. She's lived very long and seen many faces. Perhaps she can help you find him."

In a park by the cathedral, cats lounged in the shade. Some napped behind trees.

"I'm looking for someone," Carlitos told the woman named Cassandra. "Do you know this man?"

"Hmm," said Cassandra. She looked at the photo. "I know more cats than people these days. San Juan might seem small, but it's a big place. You might have to travel the whole city."

And so he did.

In a colorful plaza, old men played dominoes. Carlitos asked one man about his father . . .

then another . . . then another . . .

But no one knew his papi.

On San Sebastian Street, people wore colorful costumes and sang and danced to the rhythm of guitars.

"¡Que bonita bandera, que bonita bandera es la bandera Puertorriqueña!"

The little boy searched the faces in the crowd, but no one looked like his father.

Carlitos searched all over the city. He walked so far, he reached the edge of Old San Juan.

The castle El Morro stood at the top of a hill overlooking the bay.

"The only place left to look is that castle," Carlitos said. "Papi must be in there."

The little boy sprinted across the great lawn. His spirit felt as high as the kites in the sky.

Carlitos arrived at the steps of the castle.

"Do you know my father?" he asked the park ranger.

"Maybe," said the ranger. "What does he look like?"

The little boy reached for the photo in his pocket.

"Oh no," said Carlitos. His eyes filled with tears.
Somehow, the photo was gone!

Clouds darkened the sky. Rain poured down in buckets.
Carlitos and the ranger found shelter under an archway.

"Why are you crying?" the ranger asked Carlitos.

"I lost a photo of my father," said the boy.

"Do you remember what he looks like?" asked the ranger.

Carlitos said, "Yes."

"Then he will live forever in your memory. When sad things happen,"
the ranger said, "I think of them like dark clouds. No matter the storm,
the sun always returns."

And just like that, the rain stopped. The sun came
out and everything looked shiny and new.

Carlitos walked along the water and glanced at the town of Cataño. He wondered what his mama, his abuela, and Coco the cat were doing at that very moment.

Now the sun was beginning to set.

"Fresh azucenas!" a street vendor shouted. The little boy smiled. He handed the vendor some money and bought a fresh bouquet for Abuela.

With flowers in hand, Carlitos raced
back toward the ferry. His family was
calling from across the bay.

And Carlitos couldn't
wait to see them.